DISCARDED
VAN B DEC
W9-BMJ-156
DISCARDED

Can YOU make a SCARY FACE?

by jan thomas

beach lane books
new york london toronto sydney

Hey, you!
yes, I'm talking to you!
STAND UP!

No, I changed my mind...
SIT DOWN!

No, I changed my mind AGAIN.
STAND UP!

Okay. Are you READY?
LET'S PRETEND!

Pretend you
have a tiny bug
on your nose.
WIGGLE
IT OFF!

HA!
Hmm... It TICKLES?
WIGGLE YOUR NOSE and LAUGH!

HA!
HA!

Whoops! The tiny
TICKLY bug flew
into your mouth?

BLOW IT OUT!
COME ON, BLOW
HARDER!

Wait.
The tiny TICKLY bug is out of your mouth, but NOW it's in your SHIRT?

The only way to
GET IT OUT is to...
DO THE
CHICKEN
DANCE!

DANCE
FASTER!

The tiny TICKLY bug
is STUCK
in your shirt?

Don't worry.
PRETEND there's a
giant hungry frog coming
to eat that tiny TICKLY
bug **STUCK** in your shirt!

Ribbit.
uh-oh.

There really IS a
giant hungry frog?
SCARE HIM AWAY!

HELP!
MAKE A
SCARY FACE
NOW!

yikes!
Not THAT
scary!

Wait up,
giant hungry frog!
I'm still scared!